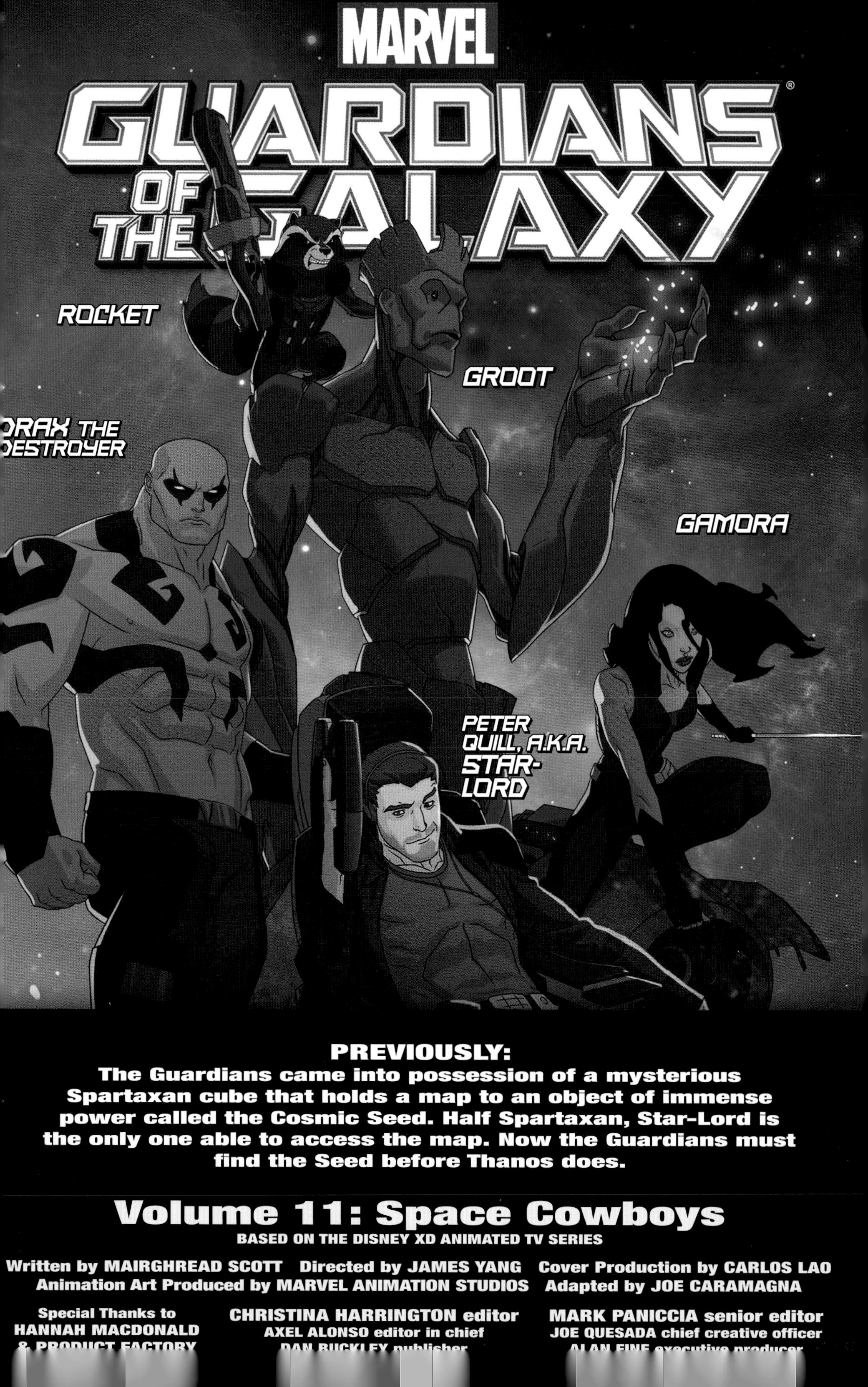
MARVEL
GUARDIANS OF THE GALAXY
ROCKET
GROOT
DRAX THE DESTROYER
GAMORA
PETER QUILL, A.K.A. STAR-LORD

PREVIOUSLY:
The Guardians came into possession of a mysterious Spartaxan cube that holds a map to an object of immense power called the Cosmic Seed. Half Spartaxan, Star-Lord is the only one able to access the map. Now the Guardians must find the Seed before Thanos does.

Volume 11: Space Cowboys

BASED ON THE DISNEY XD ANIMATED TV SERIES

Written by MAIRGHREAD SCOTT   Directed by JAMES YANG   Cover Production by CARLOS LAO
Animation Art Produced by MARVEL ANIMATION STUDIOS   Adapted by JOE CARAMAGNA

Special Thanks to HANNAH MACDONALD & PRODUCT FACTORY
CHRISTINA HARRINGTON editor
AXEL ALONSO editor in chief
DAN BUCKLEY publisher
MARK PANICCIA senior editor
JOE QUESADA chief creative officer
ALAN FINE executive producer

ABDOBOOKS.COM

Reinforced library bound edition published in 2020 by Spotlight,
a division of ABDO, PO Box 398166, Minneapolis, Minnesota 55439.
Spotlight produces high-quality reinforced library bound editions for
schools and libraries. Published by agreement with Marvel Characters, Inc.

Printed in the United States of America, North Mankato, Minnesota.
042019
092019

marvelkids.com
© 2020 MARVEL

Library of Congress Control Number: 2018965977

Publisher's Cataloging-in-Publication Data

Names: Caramagna, Joe; Scott, Mairghread, authors. | Marvel Animation Studios,
    illustrator.
Title: Space cowboys / by Joe Caramagna ; Mairghread Scott; illustrated by Marvel
    Animation Studios.
Description: Minneapolis, Minnesota : Spotlight, 2020. | Series: Guardians of the
    Galaxy Set 3 ; volume 11
Summary: The Guardians make a deal with the Collector to deliver a herd of
    Moombas in exchange for a Repulsar Generator, but they have to avoid the
    Ravagers who have been hired by the Grandmaster to take the explosive herd.
Identifiers: ISBN 9781532143625 (lib. bdg.)
Subjects: LCSH: Guardians of the Galaxy (Fictitious characters)--Juvenile fiction. |
    Superheroes--Juvenile fiction. | Cattle--Juvenile fiction. | Graphic novels--
    Juvenile fiction. | Space aliens--Juvenile fiction. | Space--Juvenile fiction. |
    Comic books, strips, etc--Juvenile fiction.
Classification: DDC 741.5--dc23

Spotlight

A Division of ABDO
abdobooks.com

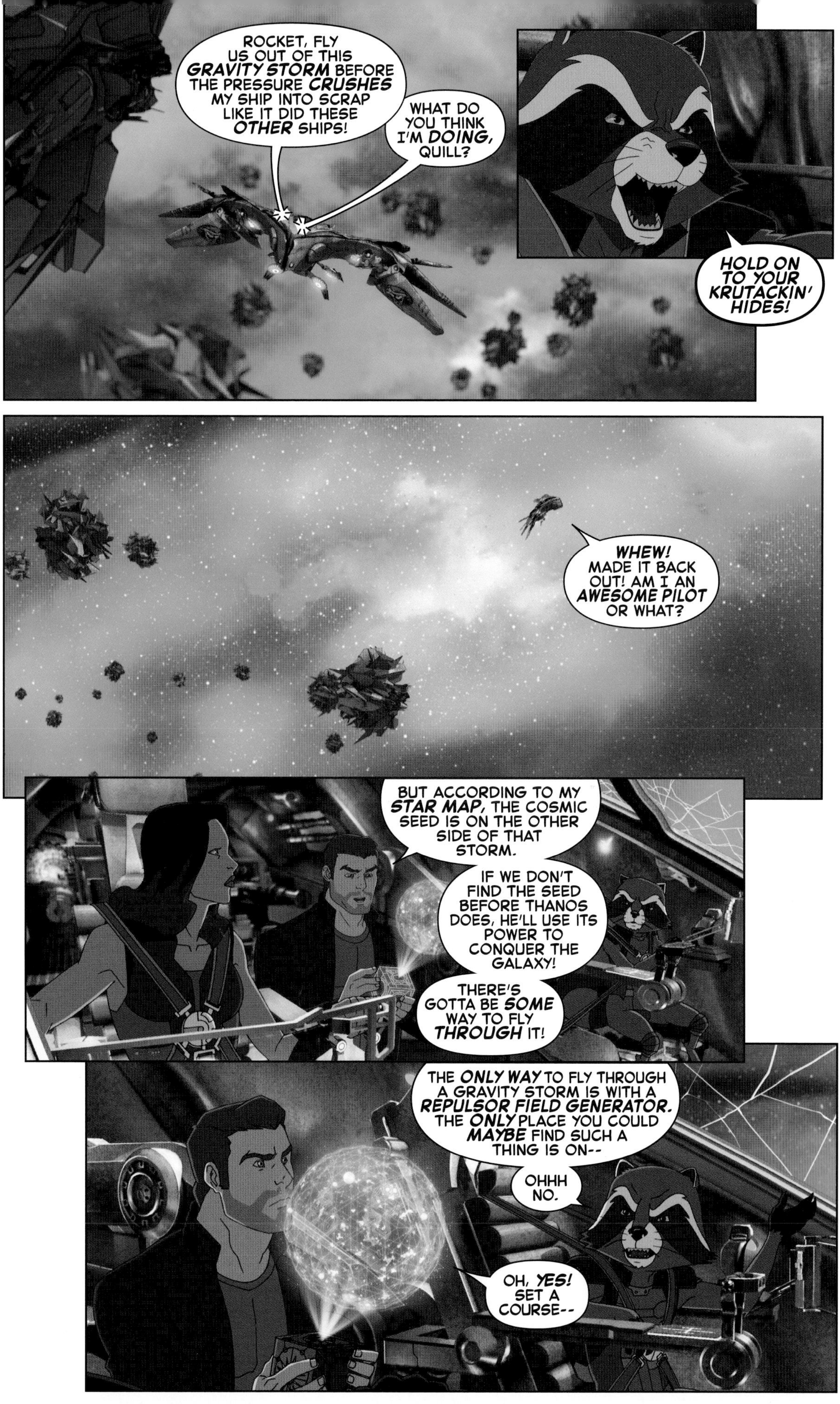
ROCKET, FLY US OUT OF THIS GRAVITY STORM BEFORE THE PRESSURE CRUSHES MY SHIP INTO SCRAP LIKE IT DID THESE OTHER SHIPS!
WHAT DO YOU THINK I'M DOING, QUILL?
HOLD ON TO YOUR KRUTACKIN' HIDES!
WHEW! MADE IT BACK OUT! AM I AN AWESOME PILOT OR WHAT?
BUT ACCORDING TO MY STAR MAP, THE COSMIC SEED IS ON THE OTHER SIDE OF THAT STORM.
IF WE DON'T FIND THE SEED BEFORE THANOS DOES, HE'LL USE ITS POWER TO CONQUER THE GALAXY!
THERE'S GOTTA BE SOME WAY TO FLY THROUGH IT!
THE ONLY WAY TO FLY THROUGH A GRAVITY STORM IS WITH A REPULSOR FIELD GENERATOR. THE ONLY PLACE YOU COULD MAYBE FIND SUCH A THING IS ON--
OHHH NO.
OH, YES! SET A COURSE--

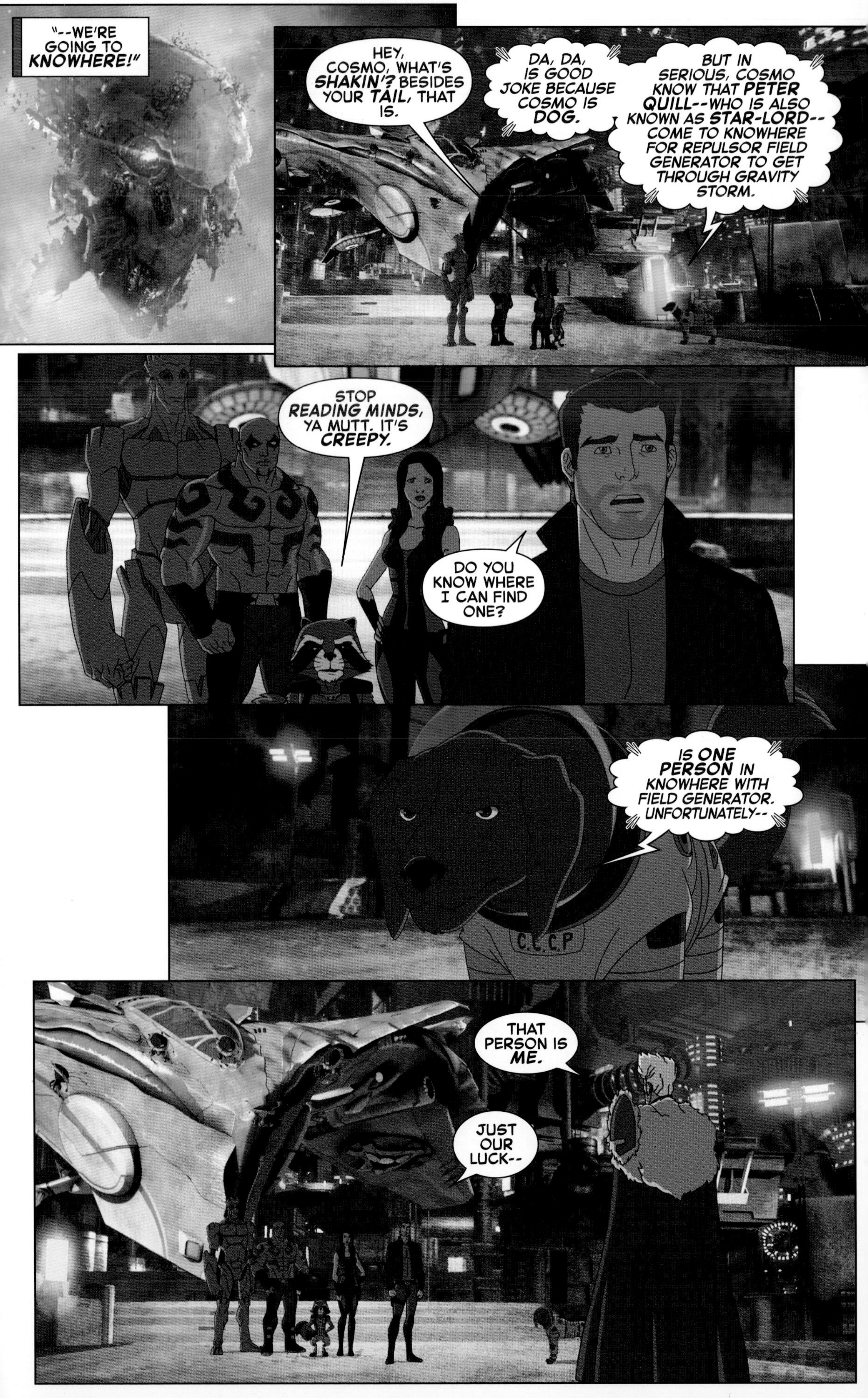
"--WE'RE GOING TO KNOWHERE!"
HEY, COSMO, WHAT'S SHAKIN'? BESIDES YOUR TAIL, THAT IS.
DA, DA, IS GOOD JOKE BECAUSE COSMO IS DOG.
BUT IN SERIOUS, COSMO KNOW THAT PETER QUILL--WHO IS ALSO KNOWN AS STAR-LORD--COME TO KNOWHERE FOR REPULSOR FIELD GENERATOR TO GET THROUGH GRAVITY STORM.
STOP READING MINDS, YA MUTT. IT'S CREEPY.
DO YOU KNOW WHERE I CAN FIND ONE?
IS ONE PERSON IN KNOWHERE WITH FIELD GENERATOR. UNFORTUNATELY--
C.C.C.P
THAT PERSON IS ME.
JUST OUR LUCK--

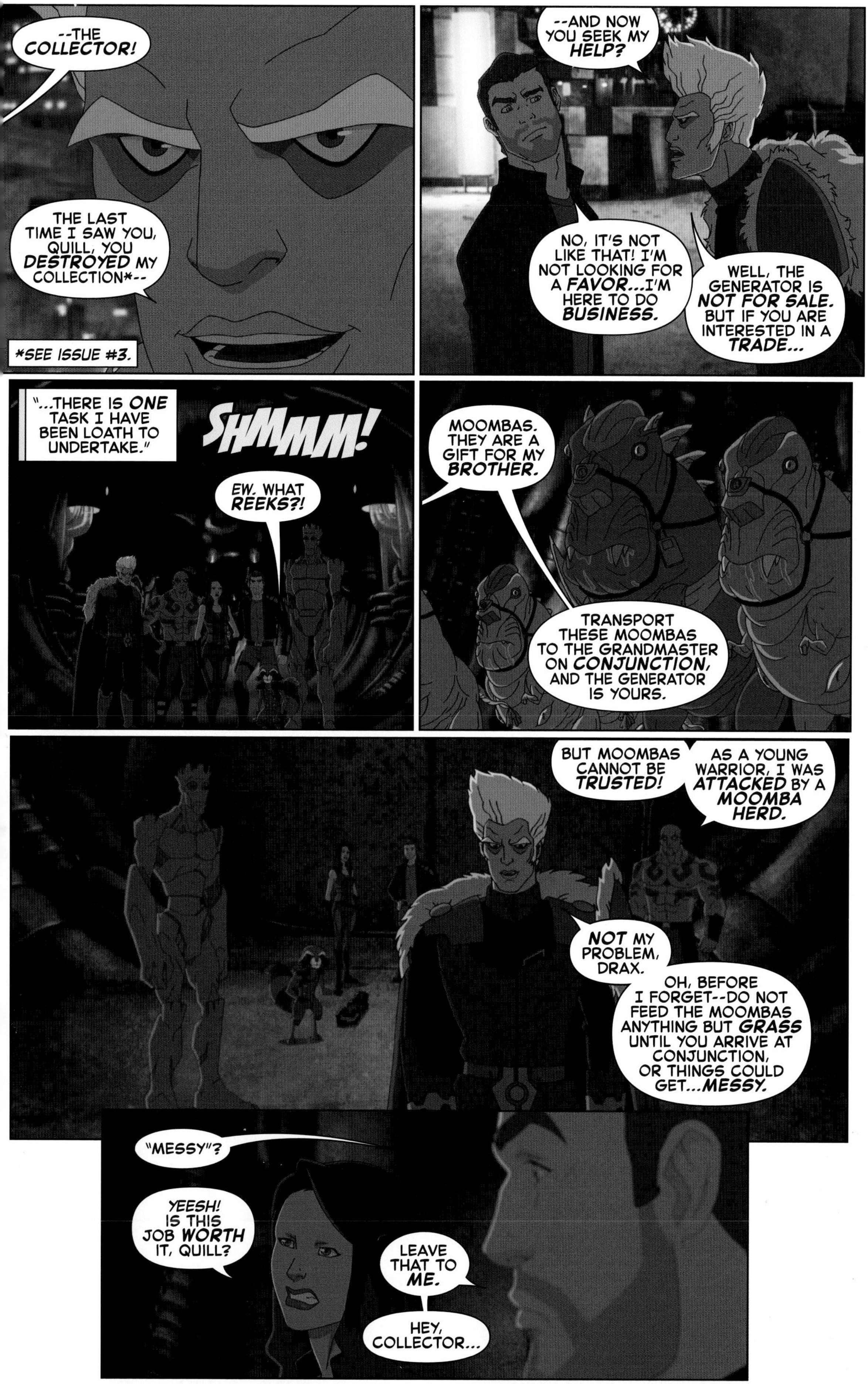
--THE COLLECTOR!
THE LAST TIME I SAW YOU, QUILL, YOU DESTROYED MY COLLECTION*--
*SEE ISSUE #3.
--AND NOW YOU SEEK MY HELP?
NO, IT'S NOT LIKE THAT! I'M NOT LOOKING FOR A FAVOR...I'M HERE TO DO BUSINESS.
WELL, THE GENERATOR IS NOT FOR SALE. BUT IF YOU ARE INTERESTED IN A TRADE...
"...THERE IS ONE TASK I HAVE BEEN LOATH TO UNDERTAKE."
SHMMM!
EW. WHAT REEKS?!
MOOMBAS. THEY ARE A GIFT FOR MY BROTHER.
TRANSPORT THESE MOOMBAS TO THE GRANDMASTER ON CONJUNCTION, AND THE GENERATOR IS YOURS.
BUT MOOMBAS CANNOT BE TRUSTED!
AS A YOUNG WARRIOR, I WAS ATTACKED BY A MOOMBA HERD.
NOT MY PROBLEM, DRAX.
OH, BEFORE I FORGET--DO NOT FEED THE MOOMBAS ANYTHING BUT GRASS UNTIL YOU ARRIVE AT CONJUNCTION, OR THINGS COULD GET...MESSY.
"MESSY"?
YEESH! IS THIS JOB WORTH IT, QUILL?
LEAVE THAT TO ME.
HEY, COLLECTOR...

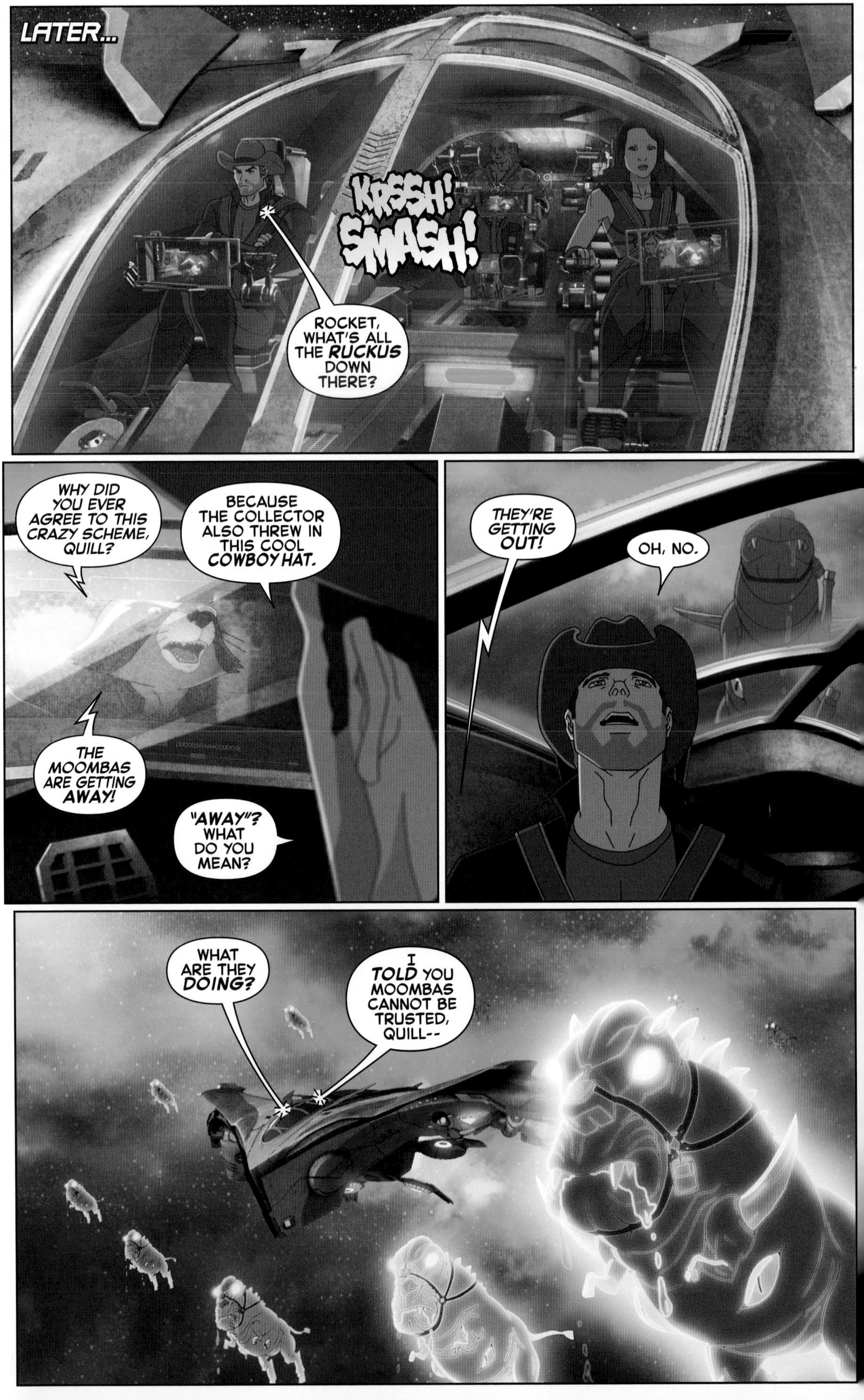

LATER...
KRSSH! SMASH!
ROCKET, WHAT'S ALL THE RUCKUS DOWN THERE?
WHY DID YOU EVER AGREE TO THIS CRAZY SCHEME, QUILL?
BECAUSE THE COLLECTOR ALSO THREW IN THIS COOL COWBOY HAT.
THE MOOMBAS ARE GETTING AWAY!
"AWAY"? WHAT DO YOU MEAN?
THEY'RE GETTING OUT!
OH, NO.
WHAT ARE THEY DOING?
I TOLD YOU MOOMBAS CANNOT BE TRUSTED, QUILL--

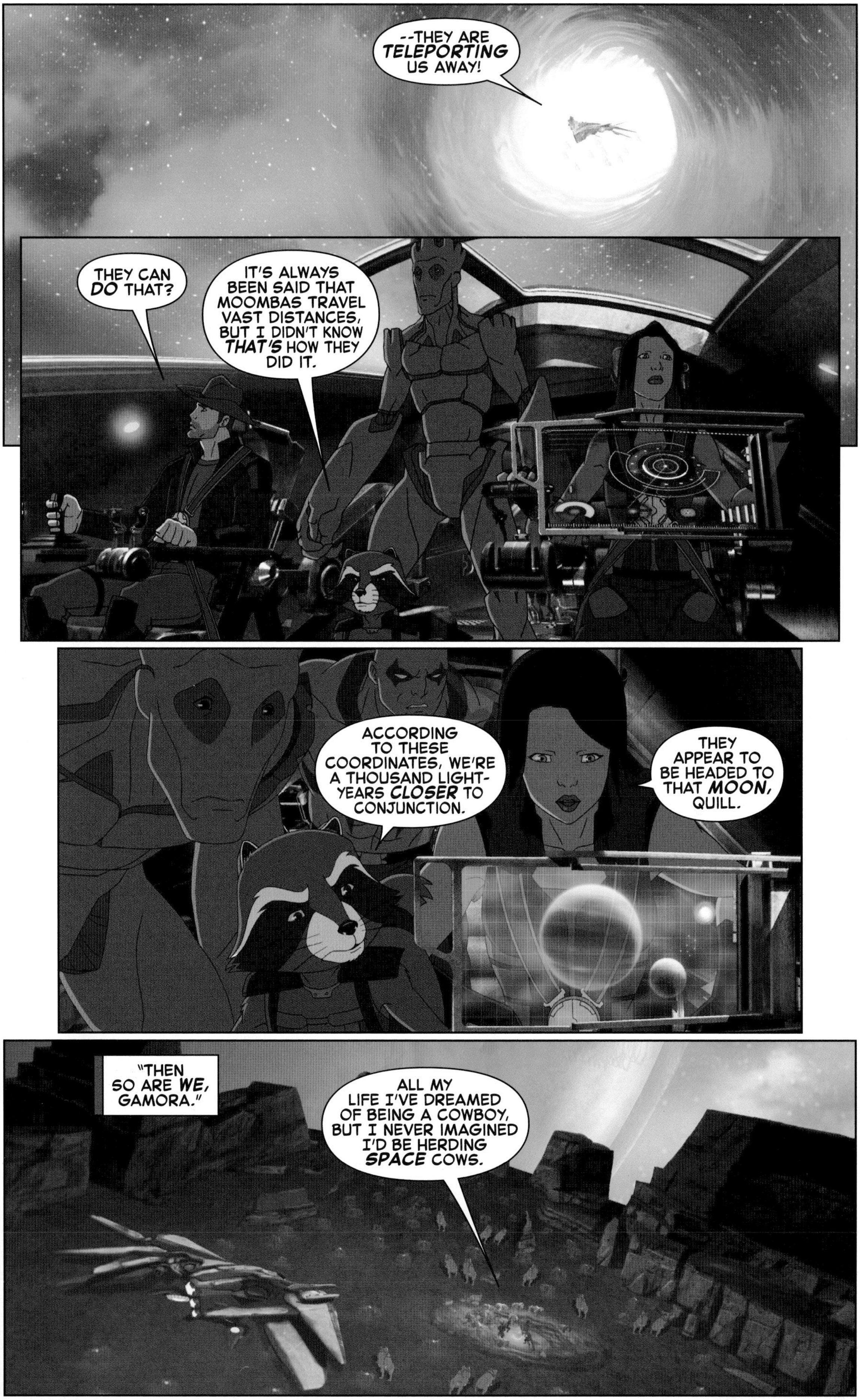
--THEY ARE TELEPORTING US AWAY!
THEY CAN DO THAT?
IT'S ALWAYS BEEN SAID THAT MOOMBAS TRAVEL VAST DISTANCES, BUT I DIDN'T KNOW THAT'S HOW THEY DID IT.
ACCORDING TO THESE COORDINATES, WE'RE A THOUSAND LIGHT-YEARS CLOSER TO CONJUNCTION.
THEY APPEAR TO BE HEADED TO THAT MOON, QUILL.
"THEN SO ARE WE, GAMORA."
ALL MY LIFE I'VE DREAMED OF BEING A COWBOY, BUT I NEVER IMAGINED I'D BE HERDING SPACE COWS.

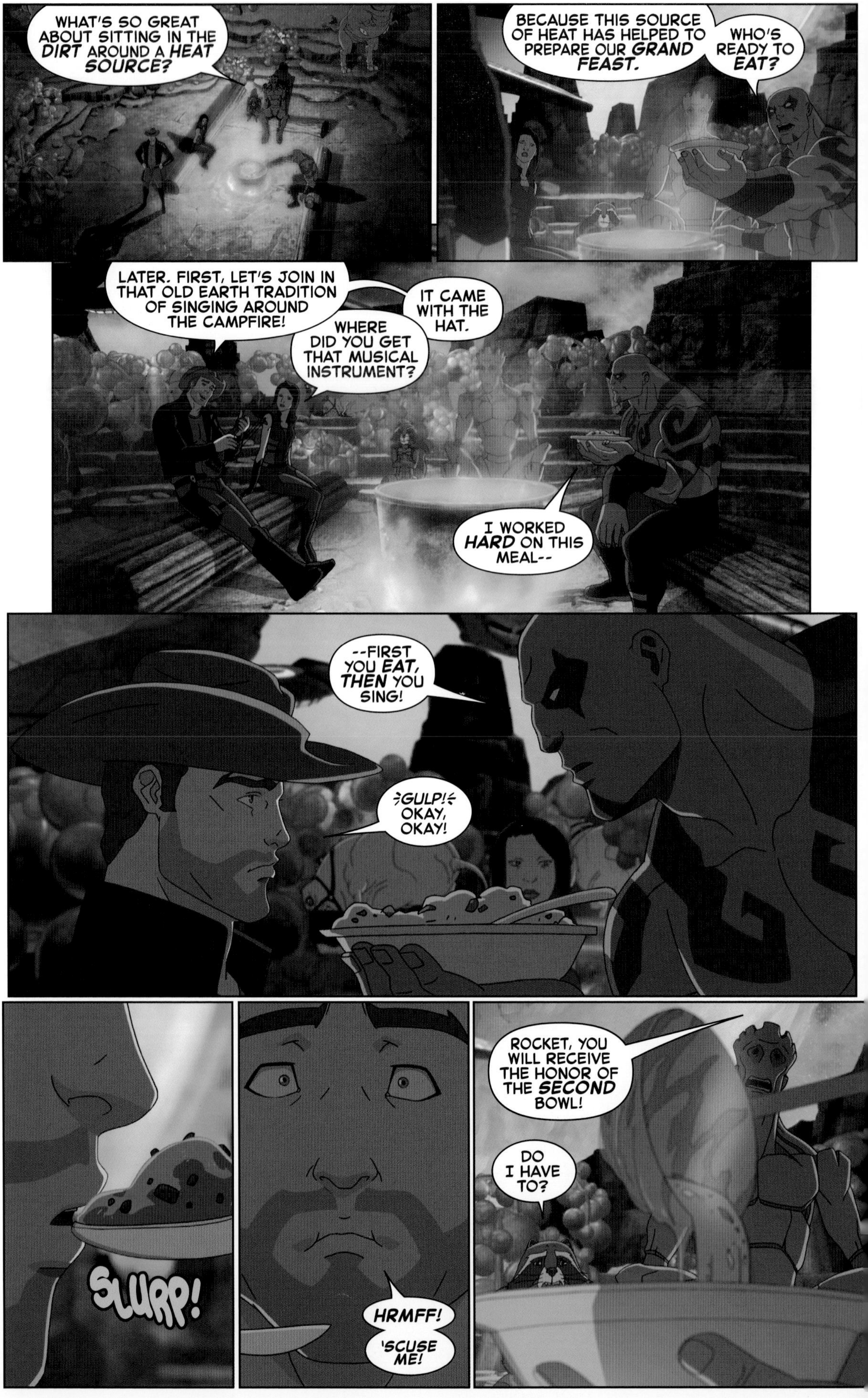
WHAT'S SO GREAT ABOUT SITTING IN THE DIRT AROUND A HEAT SOURCE?
BECAUSE THIS SOURCE OF HEAT HAS HELPED TO PREPARE OUR GRAND FEAST.
WHO'S READY TO EAT?
LATER. FIRST, LET'S JOIN IN THAT OLD EARTH TRADITION OF SINGING AROUND THE CAMPFIRE!
WHERE DID YOU GET THAT MUSICAL INSTRUMENT?
IT CAME WITH THE HAT.
I WORKED HARD ON THIS MEAL--
--FIRST YOU EAT, THEN YOU SING!
GULP! OKAY, OKAY!
SLURP!
HRMFF!
'SCUSE ME!
ROCKET, YOU WILL RECEIVE THE HONOR OF THE SECOND BOWL!
DO I HAVE TO?

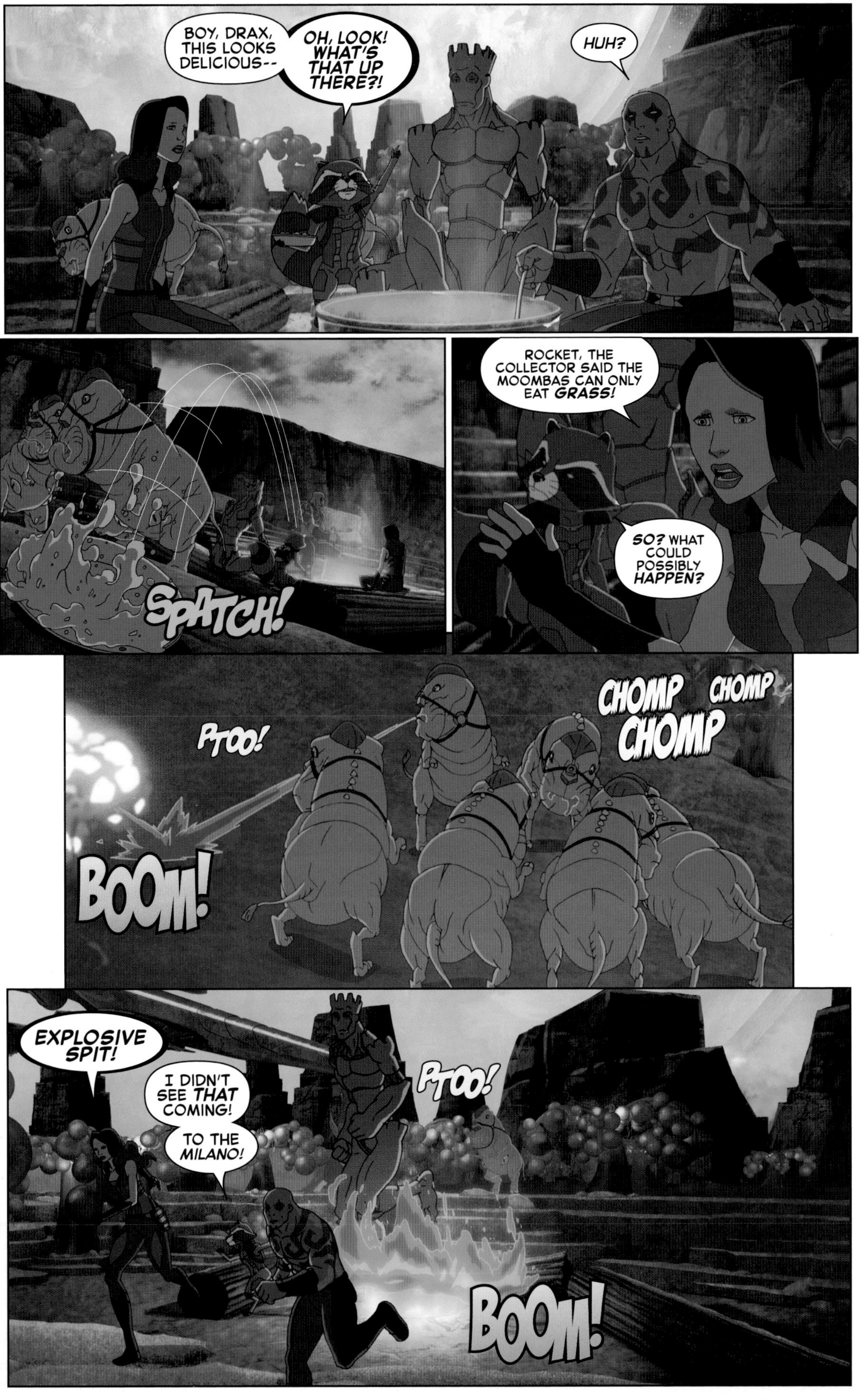
BOY, DRAX, THIS LOOKS DELICIOUS--
OH, LOOK! WHAT'S THAT UP THERE?!
HUH?
SPATCH!
ROCKET, THE COLLECTOR SAID THE MOOMBAS CAN ONLY EAT GRASS!
SO? WHAT COULD POSSIBLY HAPPEN?
PTOO!
CHOMP CHOMP
CHOMP
BOOM!
EXPLOSIVE SPIT!
I DIDN'T SEE THAT COMING!
TO THE MILANO!
PTOO!
BOOM!

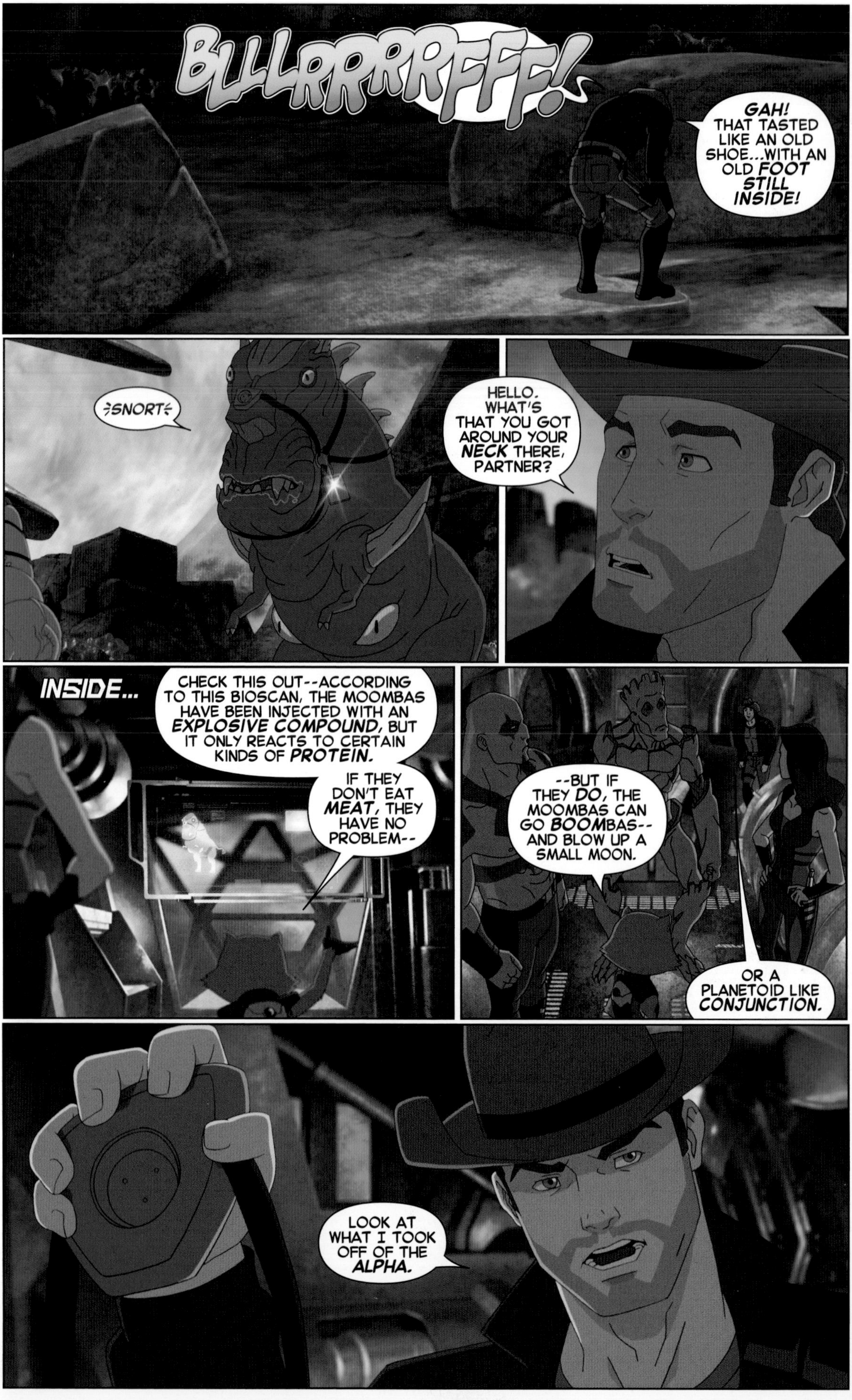
BLLLRRRRRFFF!
GAH! THAT TASTED LIKE AN OLD SHOE...WITH AN OLD FOOT STILL INSIDE!
SNORT
HELLO. WHAT'S THAT YOU GOT AROUND YOUR NECK THERE, PARTNER?
INSIDE...
CHECK THIS OUT--ACCORDING TO THIS BIOSCAN, THE MOOMBAS HAVE BEEN INJECTED WITH AN EXPLOSIVE COMPOUND, BUT IT ONLY REACTS TO CERTAIN KINDS OF PROTEIN.
IF THEY DON'T EAT MEAT, THEY HAVE NO PROBLEM--
--BUT IF THEY DO, THE MOOMBAS CAN GO BOOMBAS--AND BLOW UP A SMALL MOON.
OR A PLANETOID LIKE CONJUNCTION.
LOOK AT WHAT I TOOK OFF OF THE ALPHA.

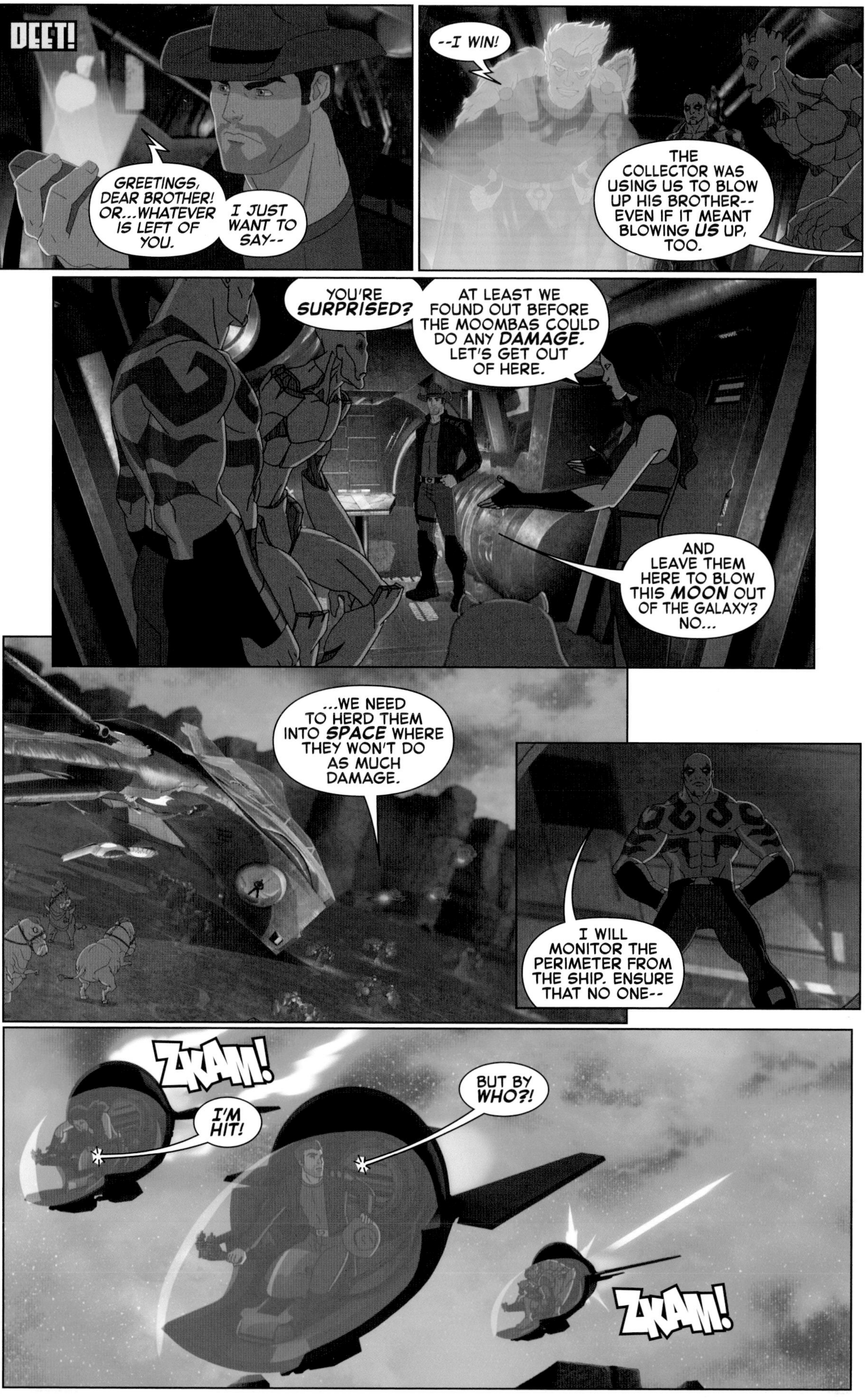
DEET!
GREETINGS, DEAR BROTHER! OR...WHATEVER IS LEFT OF YOU.
I JUST WANT TO SAY--
--I WIN!
THE COLLECTOR WAS USING US TO BLOW UP HIS BROTHER--EVEN IF IT MEANT BLOWING US UP, TOO.
YOU'RE SURPRISED?
AT LEAST WE FOUND OUT BEFORE THE MOOMBAS COULD DO ANY DAMAGE. LET'S GET OUT OF HERE.
AND LEAVE THEM HERE TO BLOW THIS MOON OUT OF THE GALAXY? NO...
...WE NEED TO HERD THEM INTO SPACE WHERE THEY WON'T DO AS MUCH DAMAGE.
I WILL MONITOR THE PERIMETER FROM THE SHIP. ENSURE THAT NO ONE--
ZKAM!
I'M HIT!
BUT BY WHO?!
ZKAM!

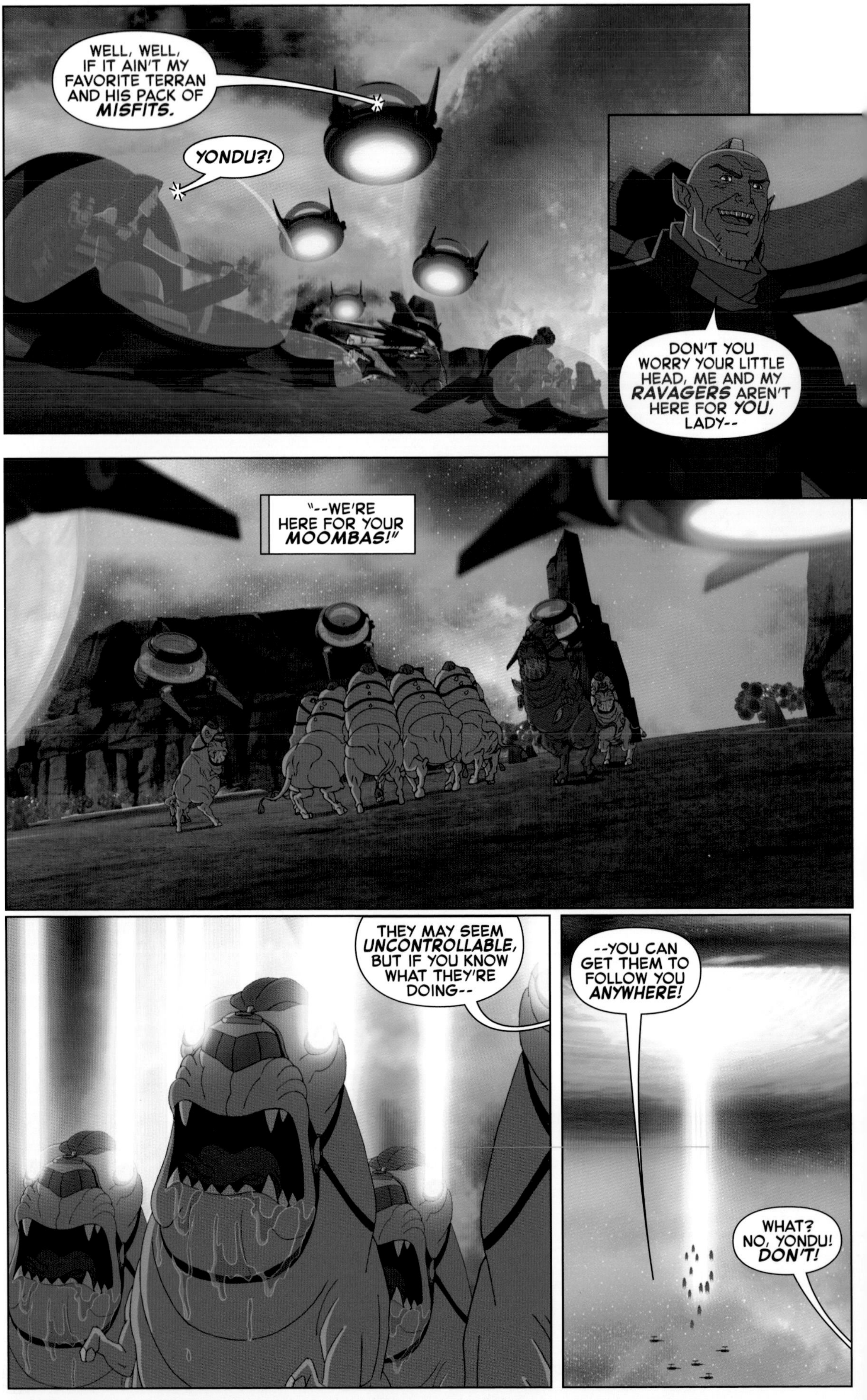
WELL, WELL, IF IT AIN'T MY FAVORITE TERRAN AND HIS PACK OF MISFITS.
YONDU?!
DON'T YOU WORRY YOUR LITTLE HEAD, ME AND MY RAVAGERS AREN'T HERE FOR YOU, LADY--
"--WE'RE HERE FOR YOUR MOOMBAS!"
THEY MAY SEEM UNCONTROLLABLE, BUT IF YOU KNOW WHAT THEY'RE DOING--
--YOU CAN GET THEM TO FOLLOW YOU ANYWHERE!
WHAT? NO, YONDU! DON'T!

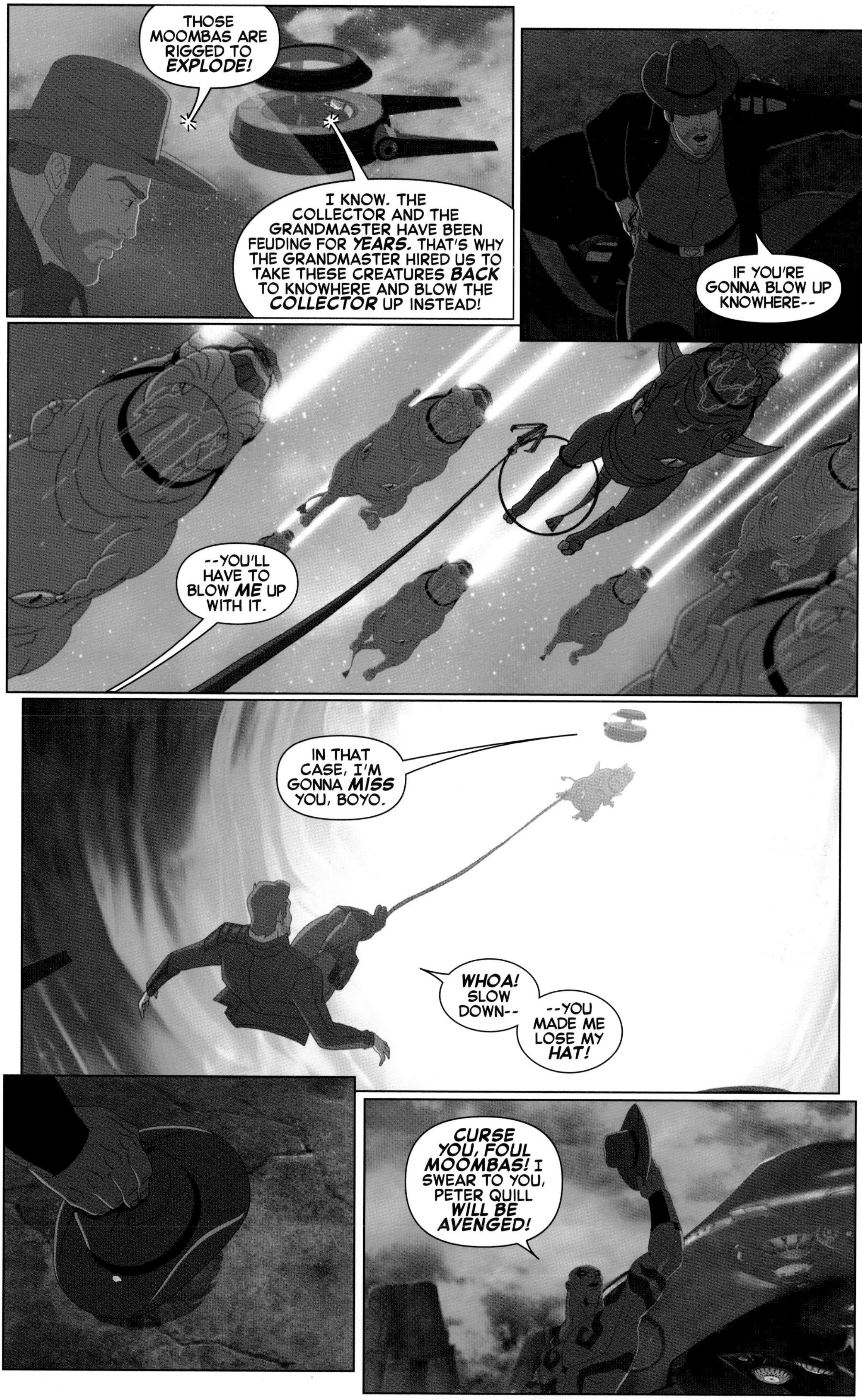
THOSE MOOMBAS ARE RIGGED TO EXPLODE!
I KNOW. THE COLLECTOR AND THE GRANDMASTER HAVE BEEN FEUDING FOR YEARS. THAT'S WHY THE GRANDMASTER HIRED US TO TAKE THESE CREATURES BACK TO KNOWHERE AND BLOW THE COLLECTOR UP INSTEAD!
IF YOU'RE GONNA BLOW UP KNOWHERE--
--YOU'LL HAVE TO BLOW ME UP WITH IT.
IN THAT CASE, I'M GONNA MISS YOU, BOYO.
WHOA! SLOW DOWN--
--YOU MADE ME LOSE MY HAT!
CURSE YOU, FOUL MOOMBAS! I SWEAR TO YOU, PETER QUILL WILL BE AVENGED!

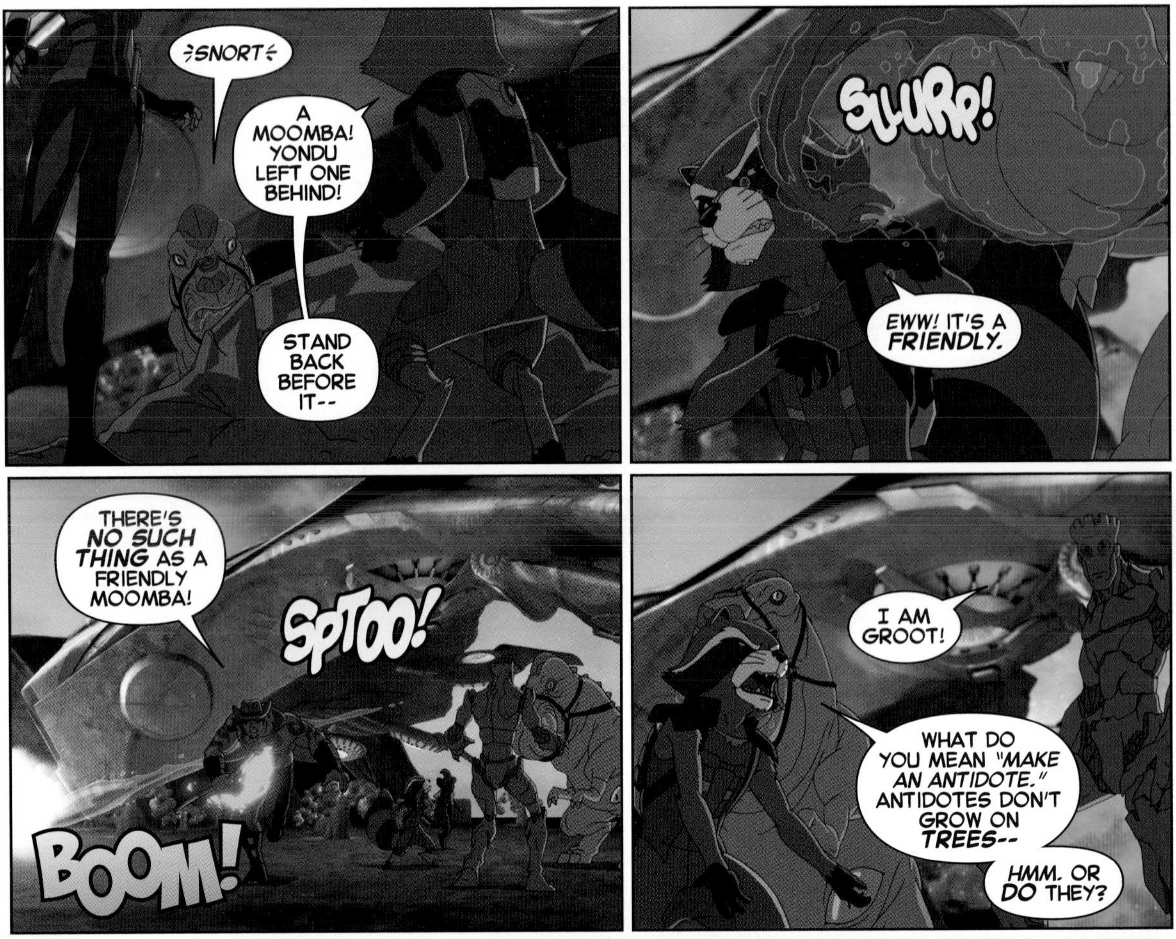
≠SNORT≠
A MOOMBA! YONDU LEFT ONE BEHIND!
STAND BACK BEFORE IT--
SLURP!
EWW! IT'S A *FRIENDLY.*
THERE'S **NO SUCH THING** AS A FRIENDLY MOOMBA!
SPTOO!
BOOM!
I AM GROOT!
WHAT DO YOU MEAN "*MAKE AN ANTIDOTE.*" ANTIDOTES DON'T GROW ON **TREES--**
HMM. OR **DO** THEY?

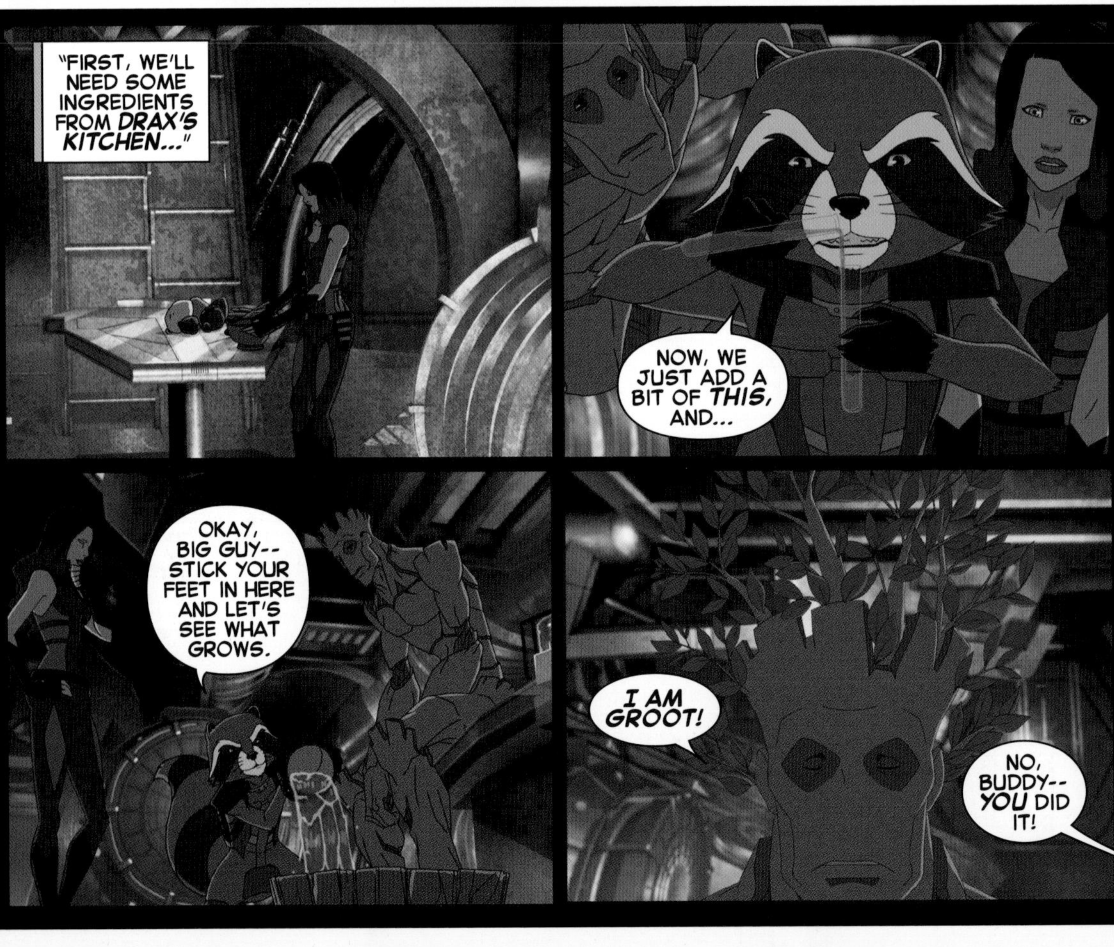
"FIRST, WE'LL NEED SOME INGREDIENTS FROM **DRAX'S KITCHEN...**"
NOW, WE JUST ADD A BIT OF **THIS,** AND...
OKAY, BIG GUY-- STICK YOUR FEET IN HERE AND LET'S SEE WHAT GROWS.
I AM GROOT!
NO, BUDDY-- **YOU** DID IT!

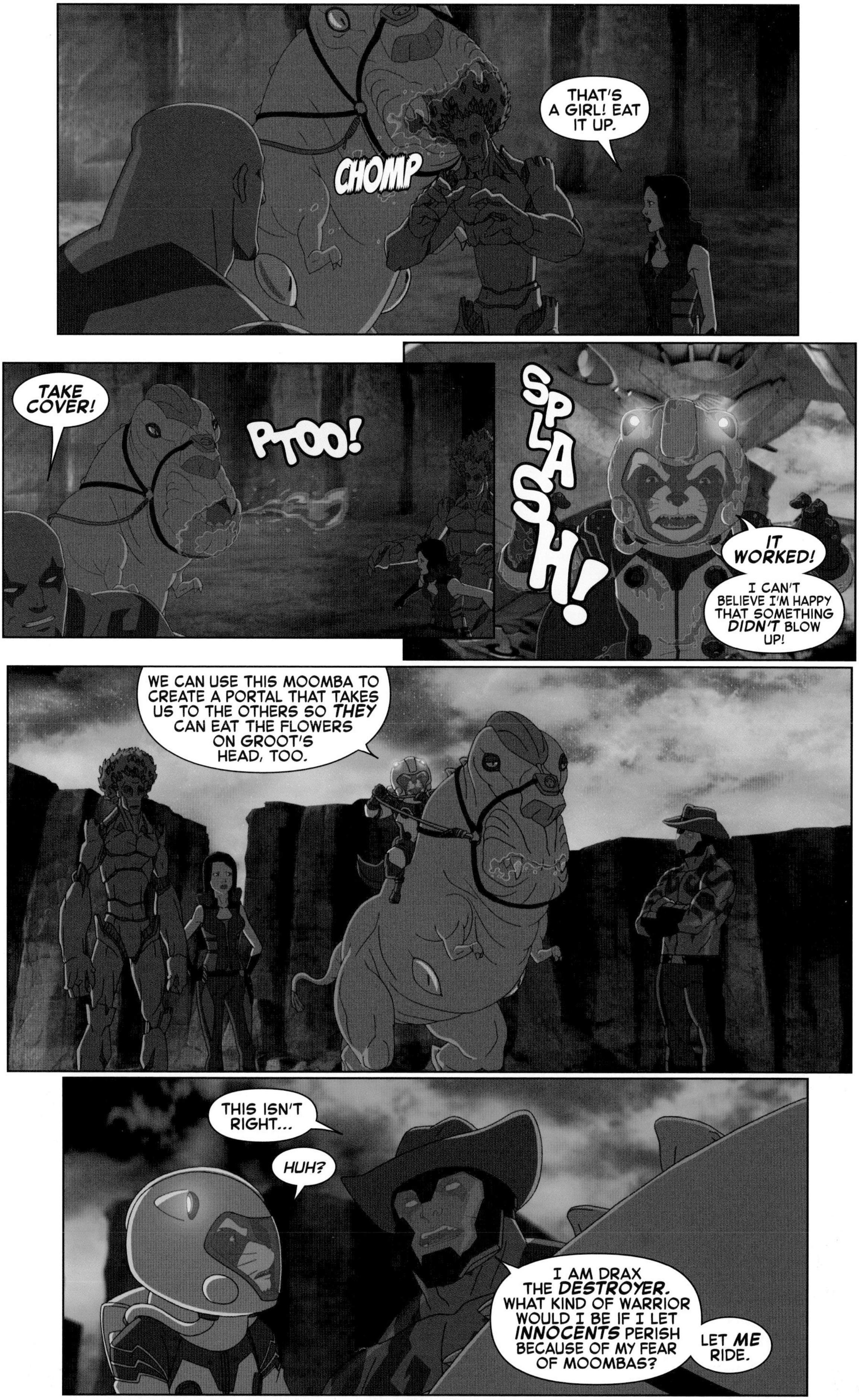

THAT'S A GIRL! EAT IT UP.
CHOMP
TAKE COVER!
PTOO!
SPLASH!
IT WORKED!
I CAN'T BELIEVE I'M HAPPY THAT SOMETHING DIDN'T BLOW UP!
WE CAN USE THIS MOOMBA TO CREATE A PORTAL THAT TAKES US TO THE OTHERS SO THEY CAN EAT THE FLOWERS ON GROOT'S HEAD, TOO.
THIS ISN'T RIGHT...
HUH?
I AM DRAX THE DESTROYER. WHAT KIND OF WARRIOR WOULD I BE IF I LET INNOCENTS PERISH BECAUSE OF MY FEAR OF MOOMBAS?
LET ME RIDE.

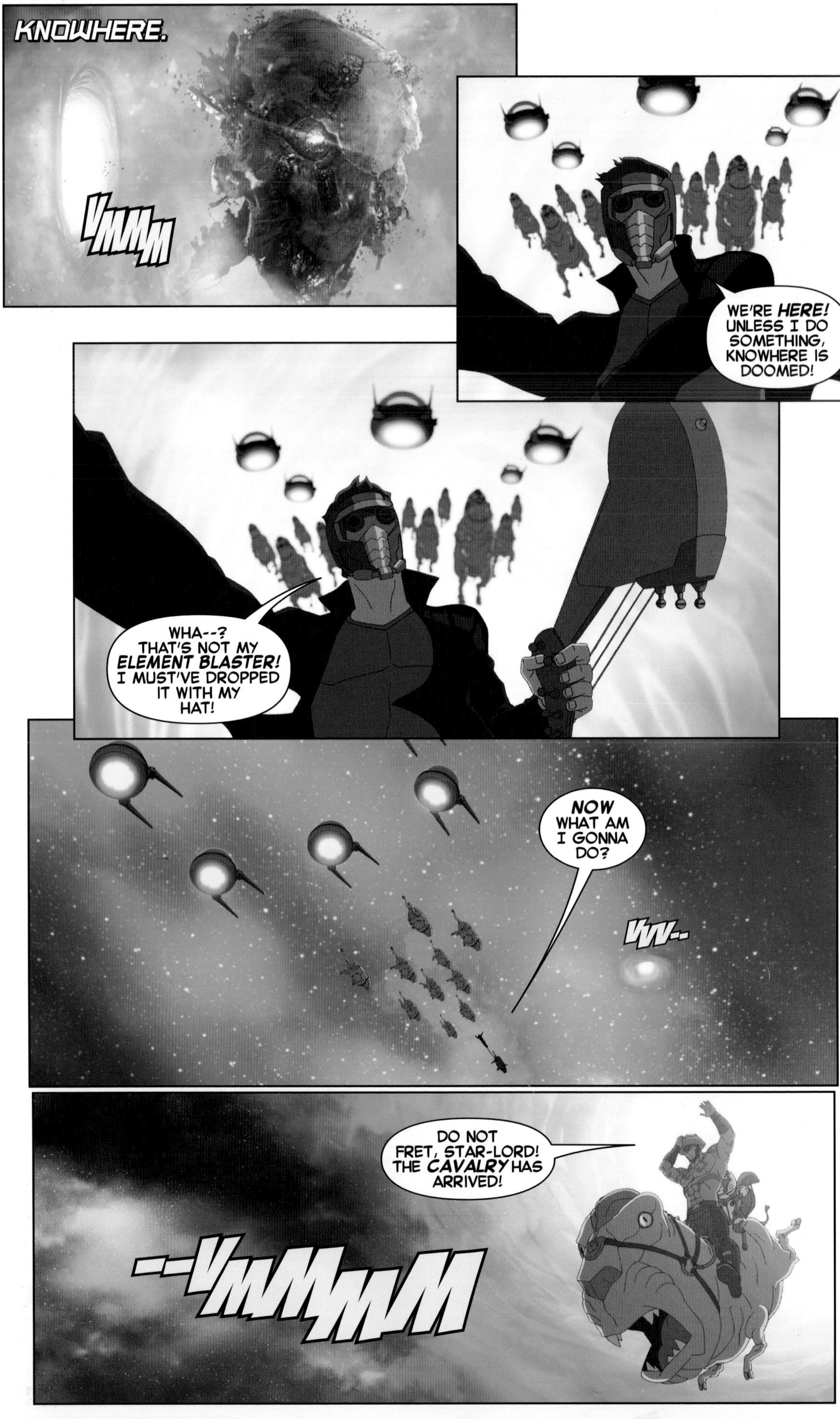
KNOWHERE.
VMMM
WE'RE HERE! UNLESS I DO SOMETHING, KNOWHERE IS DOOMED!
WHA--? THAT'S NOT MY ELEMENT BLASTER! I MUST'VE DROPPED IT WITH MY HAT!
NOW WHAT AM I GONNA DO?
VVV--
DO NOT FRET, STAR-LORD! THE CAVALRY HAS ARRIVED!
--VMMMMM

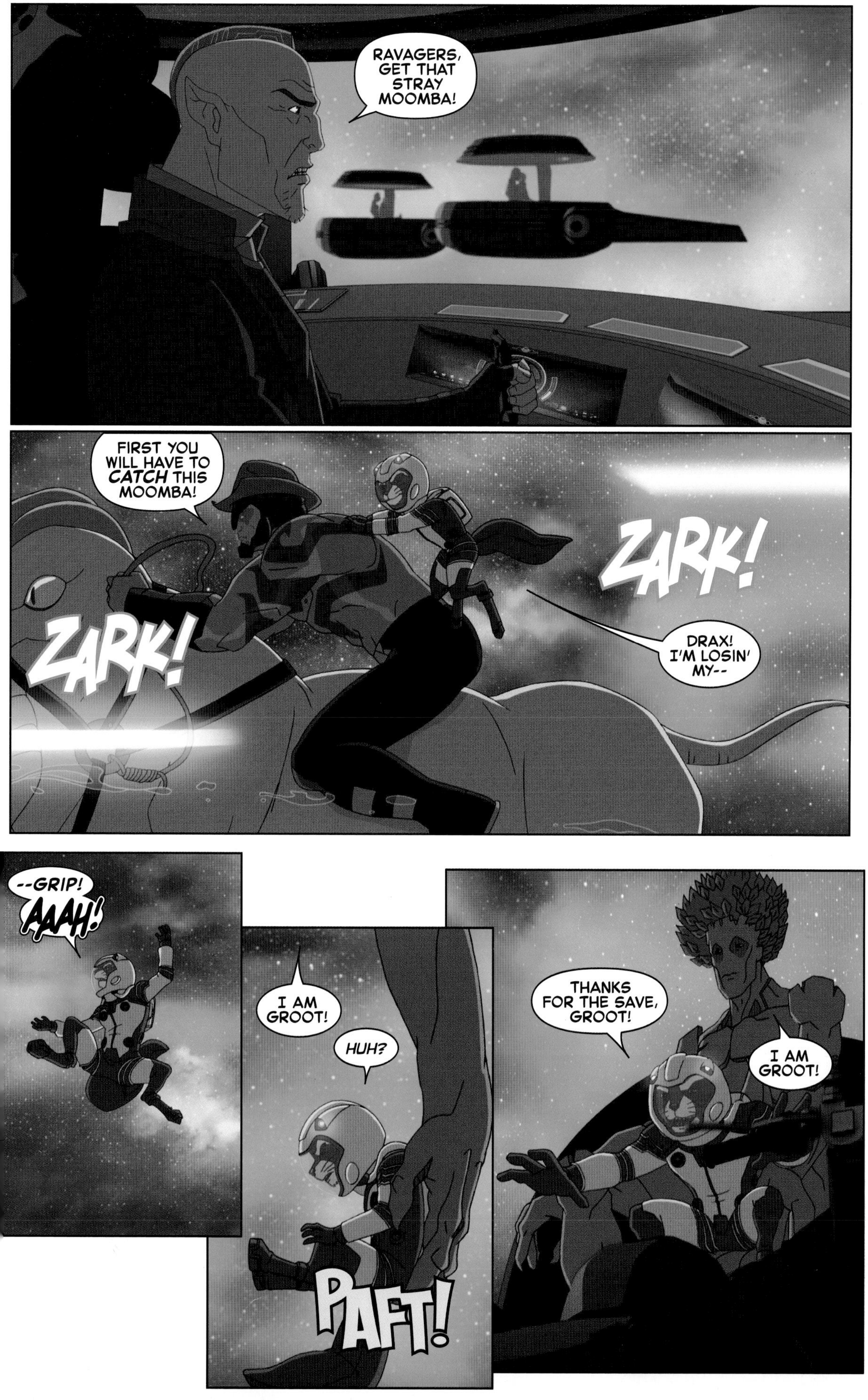
RAVAGERS, GET THAT STRAY MOOMBA!
FIRST YOU WILL HAVE TO CATCH THIS MOOMBA!
ZARK!
ZARK!
DRAX! I'M LOSIN' MY--
--GRIP!
AAAH!
I AM GROOT!
HUH?
PAFT!
THANKS FOR THE SAVE, GROOT!
I AM GROOT!

HOLD STILL, QUILL!

THIS ISN'T WHAT IT LOOKS LIKE, GAMORA!

IT LOOKS LIKE YOU'RE BEING DRAGGED BY A MOOMBA.

SLIKK!

OOOKAY, THEN IT'S EXACTLY WHAT IT LOOKS LIKE.

FASTEN YOUR SEAT BELT, GROOT. WE'RE GOIN' UPSIDE DOWN--

--'CAUSE DINNER IS SERVED!

CHOMP

CHOMP

CHOMP

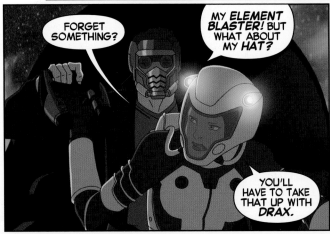

FORGET SOMETHING?

MY ELEMENT BLASTER! BUT WHAT ABOUT MY HAT?

YOU'LL HAVE TO TAKE THAT UP WITH DRAX.

FREEZE!

WHAT'S THIS NOW?

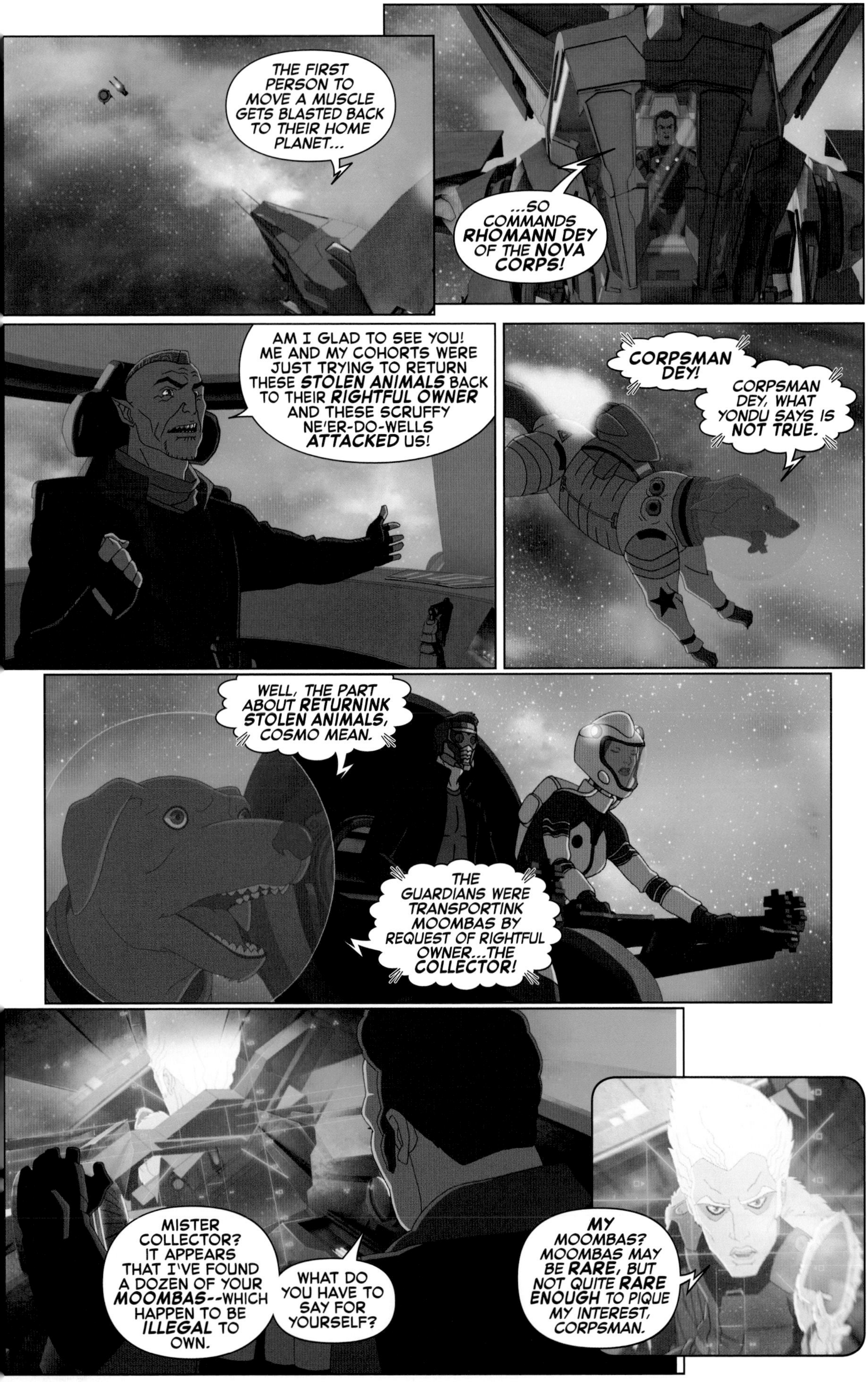
THE FIRST PERSON TO MOVE A MUSCLE GETS BLASTED BACK TO THEIR HOME PLANET...
...SO COMMANDS RHOMANN DEY OF THE NOVA CORPS!
AM I GLAD TO SEE YOU! ME AND MY COHORTS WERE JUST TRYING TO RETURN THESE STOLEN ANIMALS BACK TO THEIR RIGHTFUL OWNER AND THESE SCRUFFY NE'ER-DO-WELLS ATTACKED US!
CORPSMAN DEY!
CORPSMAN DEY, WHAT YONDU SAYS IS NOT TRUE.
WELL, THE PART ABOUT RETURNINK STOLEN ANIMALS, COSMO MEAN.
THE GUARDIANS WERE TRANSPORTINK MOOMBAS BY REQUEST OF RIGHTFUL OWNER...THE COLLECTOR!
MISTER COLLECTOR? IT APPEARS THAT I'VE FOUND A DOZEN OF YOUR MOOMBAS--WHICH HAPPEN TO BE ILLEGAL TO OWN.
WHAT DO YOU HAVE TO SAY FOR YOURSELF?
MY MOOMBAS? MOOMBAS MAY BE RARE, BUT NOT QUITE RARE ENOUGH TO PIQUE MY INTEREST, CORPSMAN.

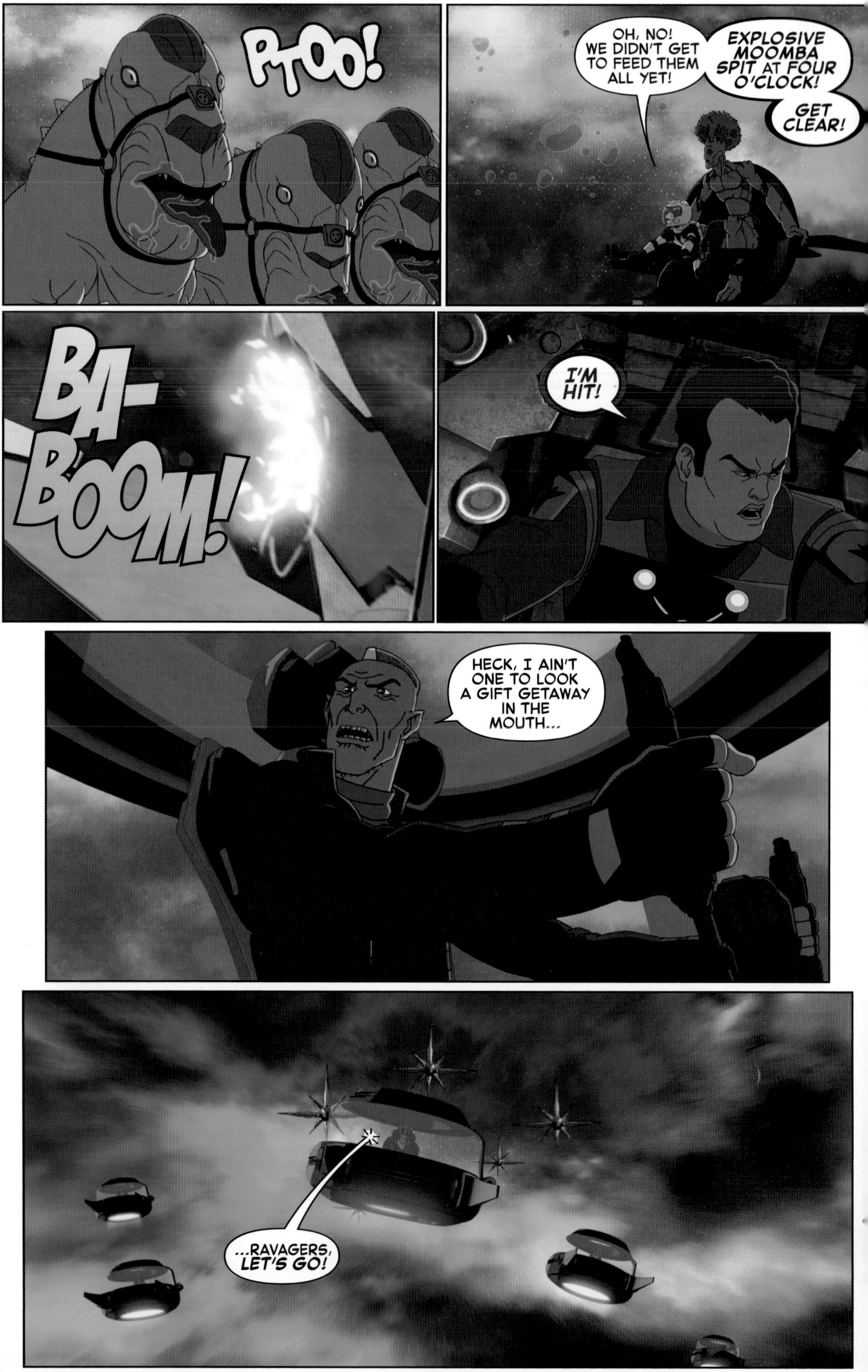
PTOO!
OH, NO! WE DIDN'T GET TO FEED THEM ALL YET!
EXPLOSIVE MOOMBA SPIT AT FOUR O'CLOCK!
GET CLEAR!
BA-BOOM!
I'M HIT!
HECK, I AIN'T ONE TO LOOK A GIFT GETAWAY IN THE MOUTH...
...RAVAGERS, LET'S GO!

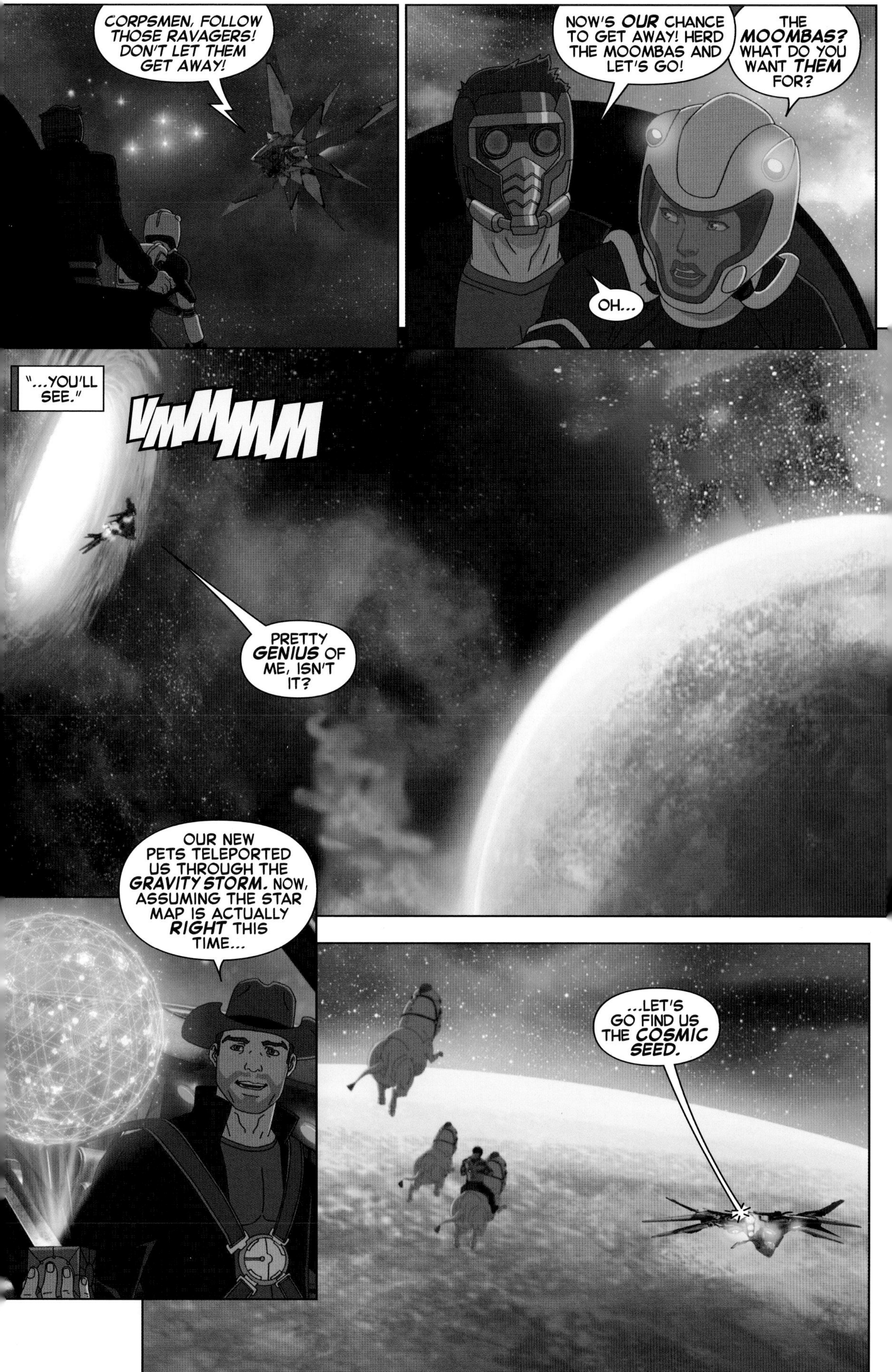
CORPSMEN, FOLLOW THOSE RAVAGERS! DON'T LET THEM GET AWAY!
NOW'S OUR CHANCE TO GET AWAY! HERD THE MOOMBAS AND LET'S GO!
THE MOOMBAS? WHAT DO YOU WANT THEM FOR?
OH...
"...YOU'LL SEE."
VMMMMM
PRETTY GENIUS OF ME, ISN'T IT?
OUR NEW PETS TELEPORTED US THROUGH THE GRAVITY STORM. NOW, ASSUMING THE STAR MAP IS ACTUALLY RIGHT THIS TIME...
...LET'S GO FIND US THE COSMIC SEED.

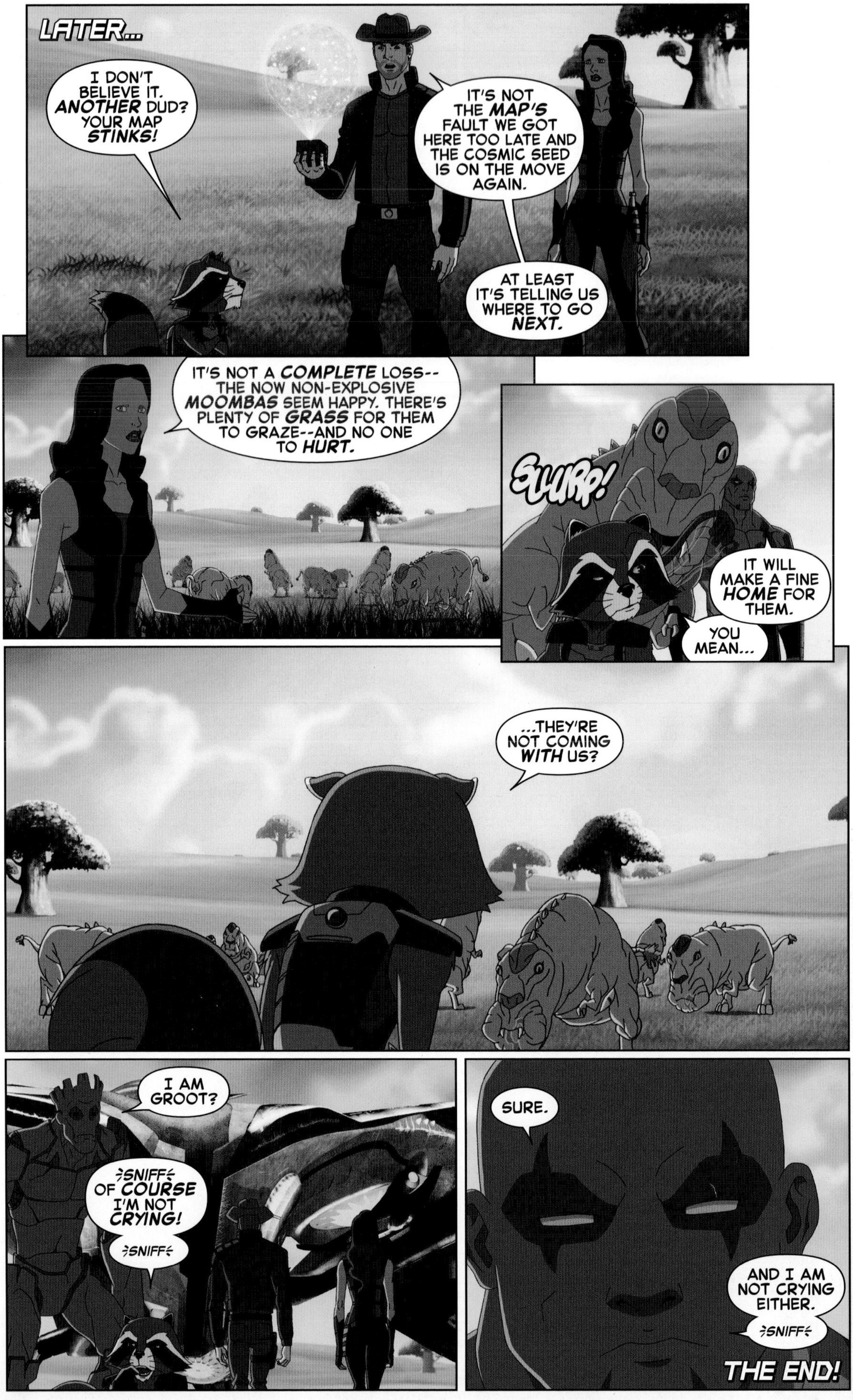
LATER...
I DON'T BELIEVE IT. ANOTHER DUD? YOUR MAP STINKS!
IT'S NOT THE MAP'S FAULT WE GOT HERE TOO LATE AND THE COSMIC SEED IS ON THE MOVE AGAIN.
AT LEAST IT'S TELLING US WHERE TO GO NEXT.
IT'S NOT A COMPLETE LOSS-- THE NOW NON-EXPLOSIVE MOOMBAS SEEM HAPPY. THERE'S PLENTY OF GRASS FOR THEM TO GRAZE--AND NO ONE TO HURT.
SLLURP!
IT WILL MAKE A FINE HOME FOR THEM.
YOU MEAN...
...THEY'RE NOT COMING WITH US?
I AM GROOT?
SNIFF OF COURSE I'M NOT CRYING!
SNIFF
SURE.
AND I AM NOT CRYING EITHER.
SNIFF
THE END!

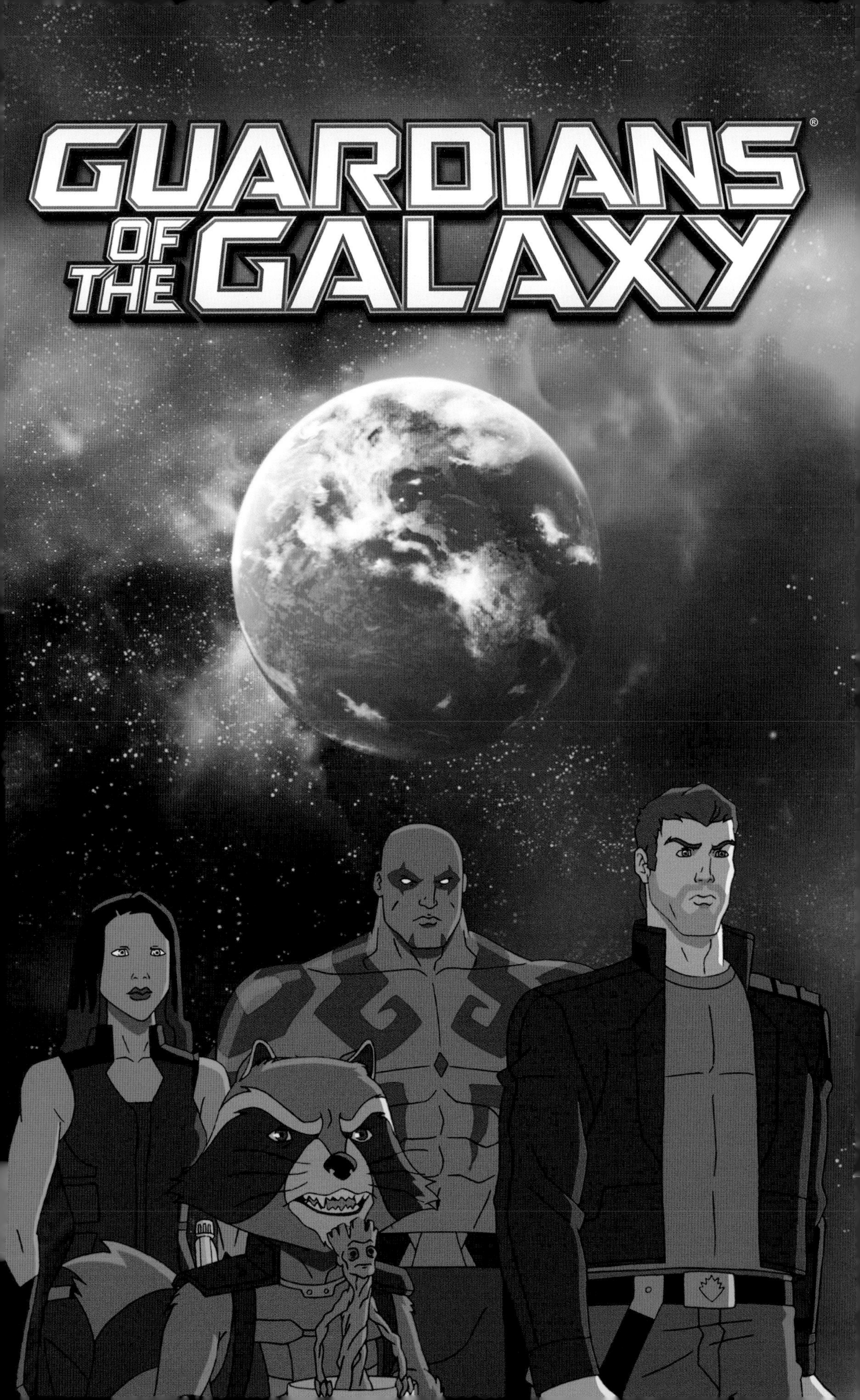
GUARDIANS OF THE GALAXY®

GUARDIANS OF THE GALAXY®

COLLECT THEM ALL!

Set of 6 Hardcover Books ISBN: 978-1-5321-4357-1

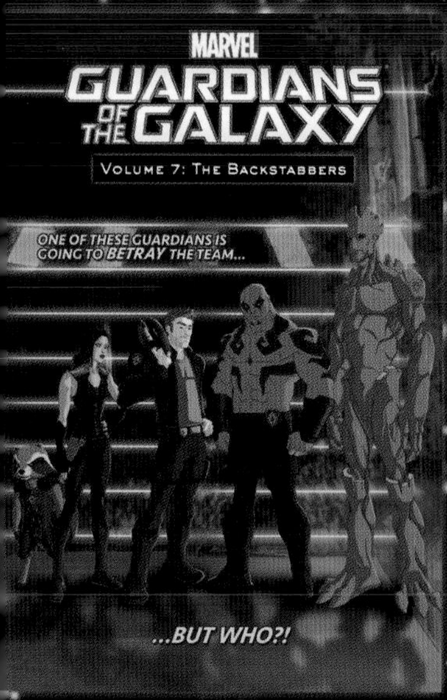
MARVEL
GUARDIANS OF THE GALAXY
VOLUME 7: THE BACKSTABBERS
ONE OF THESE GUARDIANS IS GOING TO BETRAY THE TEAM...
...BUT WHO?!

Hardcover Book ISBN
978-1-5321-4358-8

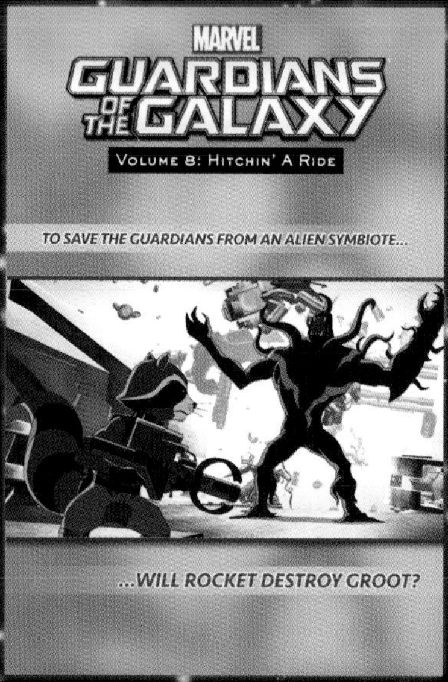
MARVEL
GUARDIANS OF THE GALAXY
VOLUME 8: HITCHIN' A RIDE
TO SAVE THE GUARDIANS FROM AN ALIEN SYMBIOTE...
...WILL ROCKET DESTROY GROOT?

Hardcover Book ISBN
978-1-5321-4359-5

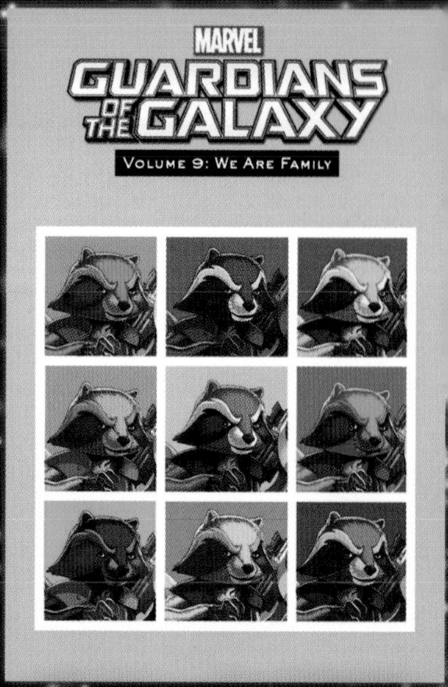
MARVEL
GUARDIANS OF THE GALAXY
VOLUME 9: WE ARE FAMILY

Hardcover Book ISBN
978-1-5321-4360-1

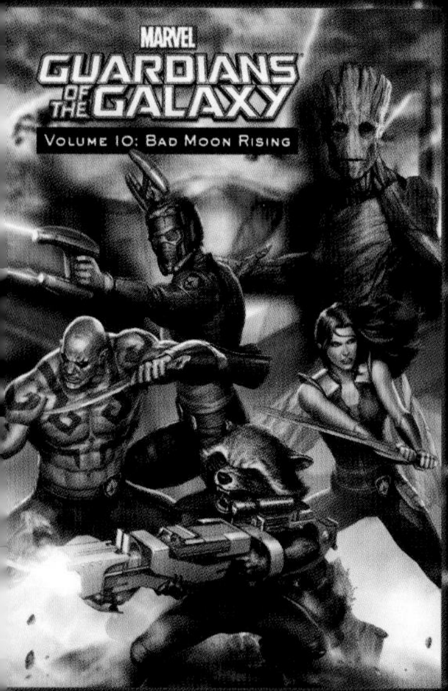
MARVEL
GUARDIANS OF THE GALAXY
VOLUME 10: BAD MOON RISING

Hardcover Book ISBN
978-1-5321-4361-8

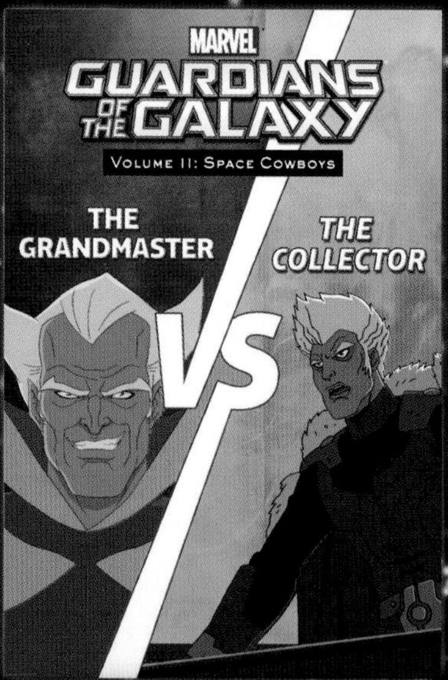
MARVEL
GUARDIANS OF THE GALAXY
VOLUME 11: SPACE COWBOYS
THE GRANDMASTER
THE COLLECTOR
VS

Hardcover Book ISBN
978-1-5321-4362-5

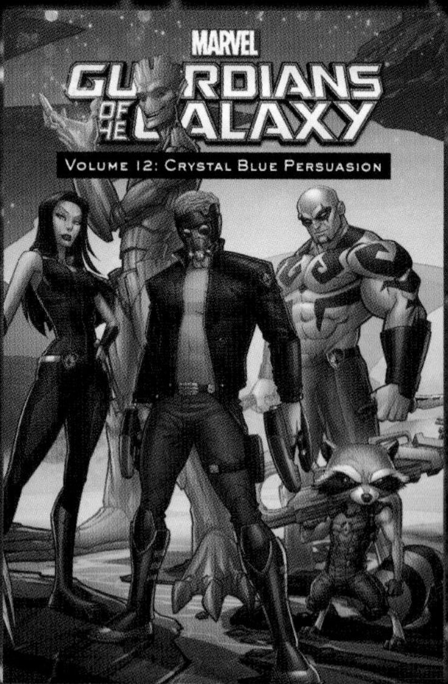
MARVEL
VOLUME 12: CRYSTAL BLUE PERSUASION

Hardcover Book ISBN
978-1-5321-4363-2